COUNT WORM

Roger Hargreaves

Publishers · GROSSET & DUNLAP · New York

Library of Congress Catalog Card Number: 81-84547
ISBN: 0-448-12318-5

First published in Great Britain by Hodder and Stoughton.
Published in the United States by Ottenheimer Publishers, Inc.
Published simultaneously in Canada.

COUNT WORM

Once there was a worm.

One morning, when Count Worm was out for a walk,
or rather a crawl, he met a small boy.
The boy was crying.
"What's the matter?"
asked Count Worm kindly.
"Why are you crying?"
"Because I can't count,"
sniffled the boy.

"Now, now," said Count Worm.
"Would you like me to teach you how to count?"
"Oh, yes, please," said the boy and stopped crying.
"Very well," said
Count Worm. "Let
us begin."

"Now," continued Count Worm, "let me ask you a question. How many noses do you have on your face?" The boy tried to look at his nose.

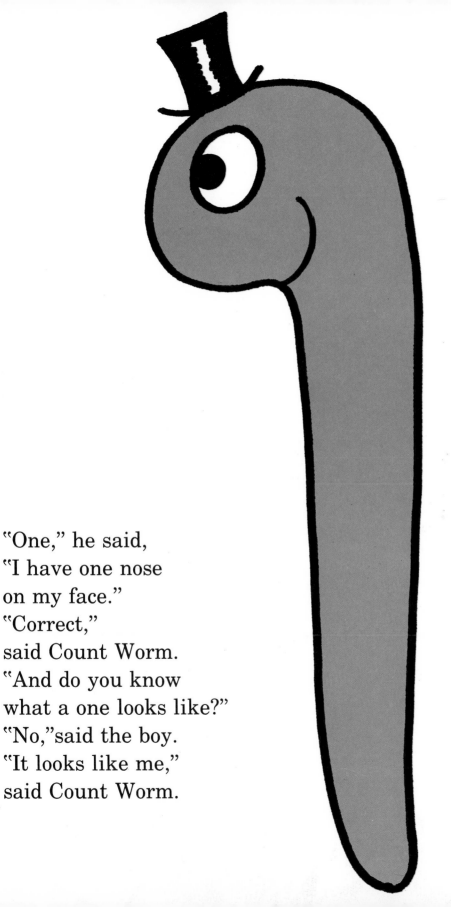

"One," he said,
"I have one nose
on my face."
"Correct,"
said Count Worm.
"And do you know
what a one looks like?"
"No,"said the boy.
"It looks like me,"
said Count Worm.

"Now," he continued, "let me ask you another
question. How many feet do you have?"
The boy looked down at his feet.
It was easier than trying to look at his nose!
"I have two feet," he replied.

"Correct," said Count Worm.
"You do indeed have two
feet. In fact, you have two
feet more than me!"

And he turned himself into a two.
"Is that what a two looks like?"
asked the boy.
"Absolutely," smiled Count Worm.

"And what comes after two?" asked Count Worm.
"Don't know," said the boy.
"Three," said Count Worm. "Three comes after
two, and two comes after one."
"Oh," said the boy.
"Look over there," said Count Worm. "In that
field there are three trees."

And he turned himself
into a three.
"One, two, three,"
said the boy.
"Correct," replied
Count Worm.

"And then comes four," he continued.
"Look, there are four birds sitting on that
branch. Count them."
"One, two, three, four," counted the boy.

"Excellent," smiled Count Worm, who had already become a four.

They came to a fence.
"How many bars does that fence have?" asked Count Worm.
The boy climbed up the fence.
"One, two, three, four, five."

"And this is what a five looks like," said Count Worm.

They climbed over the fence and came to a field.
"How many clouds are there in the sky?" asked Count Worm.
"One, two, three, four, five, er . . . what comes next?"
asked the boy.

"Six," replied Count Worm.

At the other side of the field was a farmhouse.
"How many doors?" asked Count Worm.
"One," said the boy.
"And how many chimneys?"
"Two," said the boy.
"Correct," replied Count Worm.

"How many windows does it have?"
asked the boy.
"One, two, three, four, five,
six, seven," said Count Worm.

"After seven comes eight," said Count Worm. "One, two, three, four, five, six, seven, eight. Like the flowers over there." "One, two, three, four, five, six, seven, eight flowers," said the boy.

"Look," said Count Worm, "there are nine apples on that apple tree!" "No there aren't," said the boy, and he picked one of the apples and ate it! "Now there are only eight apples," he said, with his mouth full.

Count Worm smiled as
he turned himself
into a nine.
"You've learned how
to count," he said,
and laughed.

"One, two, three, four, five, six, seven,
eight, nine," said the boy.
"What comes after nine?"
"Ten," replied Count Worm.
"Will you turn yourself into a ten for me?"
asked the boy.

"Sorry," said Count
Worm, "I can't do that
without the help of
a friend."
And he whistled
a very loud worm
whistle.

Another worm appeared out of the ground.
"Percy," said Count Worm, for that was the
other worm's name, "will you help me show
this little boy what a ten looks like?"
"My pleasure," said Percy.

And between them they made a ten.
"Thank you very much, Percy," said the boy.
"My pleasure," replied Percy and disappeared
into the ground.
And then the boy also said, "Thank you," to
Count Worm.
And then he went home saying: "One, two, three,
four, five, six, seven, eight, nine, ten,"
over and over to himself.

Count Worm smiled . . .

. . . and crawled off.